DINO RIDERS

How to Hog-Tie a T-Rex

Don't miss:

How to Tame a Triceratops

How to Rope a Giganotosaurus

How to Catch a Dino Thief

DINO RIDERS

How to Hog-Tie a T-Rex

Will Dare

sourcebooks
jabberwocky

Published by Sourcebooks Jabberwocky, an imprint of Sourcebooks, Inc.
P.O. Box 4410, Naperville, Illinois 60567-4410
(630) 961-3900
Fax: (630) 961-2168
www.sourcebooks.com

Library of Congress Cataloging-in-Publication data is on file with the publisher.

Printed and bound in the United States of America.
VP 10 9 8 7 6 5 4 3 2 1

With special thanks to Barry Hutchison.

CHAPTER 1

Josh Sanders and his best friends, Sam and Abi, held their breath as an iguanodon loudly *parped* a cloud of toxic gas in front of them. They were trotting along on their dinosaurs: Sam and Abi were riding their trusty gallimimuses, while Josh rocked in the saddle of Charge, his triceratops.

Overhead, the afternoon sun blazed down. Before them, a thousand iguanodons plodded their way across a vast, barren plain, headed for the snow-topped Wandering Mountains a few miles ahead.

Once a year, Josh and his friends would join half the adults in Trihorn settlement on the iguanodon drive out to Scaly Point. A rancher could make a lot of money selling guanos at Scaly Point, and although it meant a three-week round-trip, Josh loved every minute of it.

Well, *most* minutes of it. Iguanodons were smelly beasts at the best of times, and being stuck behind a thousand of them sure made his eyes water.

"So today is day seven, right?" asked Abi, trotting along on Josh's left.

2

The Journey So Far:

DAY 1: Head out with the herd.

DAY 2: Splodge through the Scratchclaw Swamps. Lose a shoe in the quicksand.

DAY 3: Sneak through Cold Fear Forest. Almost get eaten by a dragonfly the size of my head.

DAY 4: Survive stampeding iguanodons.

DAY 5: Survive iguanodon stink cloud.

DAY 6: Arrive at the staging post to gather vital supplies. Get new shoe.

"Uh, I think so," Josh replied, flicking through his notebook to make sure.

"Correct," said Sam over on Josh's right. "By the end of today, we will officially be one-third of the way through the journey."

"Only a week until we reach Scaly Point," said Josh.

"Only?" Abi groaned. "My saddle sores have saddle sores. I reckon that bed back at the staging post was made of razor wire and rocks."

"True," Sam said and nodded. "The beds were lousy, but there was one thing the staging post was good for…" He reached into his overflowing saddlebags and pulled out a colorful paper bag. "Candy!"

Josh and Abi both laughed.

"That's not all candy in there, is it?" asked Josh.

"Indeed it is," said Sam. "You can never have too much!"

"I think the dentist might disagree with you," said Abi.

"Yes, but he's not here," Sam replied. "Try this stuff. It's amazing!"

He reached across and poured some shimmering yellow powder from the bag into Josh's hand. Josh passed some across to Abi, and they both tipped the powder into their mouths at the same time. At first, nothing happened. The powder tasted OK, but it was nothing special. Josh was about to say as much when he felt a tingling on his tongue.

"What the—" he began. But before he finished, the powder fizzed against his gums. His eyes went wide. His lips went tight. He gasped, and his face twisted up as an explosion of sourness went *pop-pop-pop* inside his mouth. It tasted partly like lemon, partly like lime, and partly like the powder Josh's mom used to do the laundry, and it jumped around inside his mouth like a diplodocus playing hopscotch.

Josh glanced at Abi,

whose face was also twisted up. They both opened their mouths at the same time, and lots of fizzing yellow foam dribbled down their chins.

"What is that stuff?" Abi asked as she gasped.

"It's called Tasty TNT popping candy!" He laughed as he tucked the bag back into his saddle. "Good, isn't it?"

"Great," Josh said with a wheeze. "It nearly blew my head off!"

There was a thunder of dino feet beside them, and Josh's dad rode up. He took one look at Abi and Josh and asked, "Something happen to your faces?"

"Tasty TNT," Josh said. "Don't ask."

Dad nodded and tipped his hat back. "Fair enough. There's a narrow pass through the mountains up ahead. Reckon I'll go help lead from the front and try to squeeze the guanos through. You OK hanging back here to watch for stragglers?"

Josh touched the brim of his hat. "Sure thing, Dad."

"Attaboy," Dad said, leaning across and patting his son on the shoulder. "Knew I could count on you three. Yah!"

He kicked with his heels, and his dinosaur sprang forward. Josh watched him weave and dodge through the iguanodon herd until he was lost in the clouds of dust and sand churned up by the animals' heavy feet.

Sam sighed. "We couldn't be up front. We had to be back here at the smelly end."

As if on cue, an iguanodon right in front of him raised a back leg.

"Oh, hey, I picked up something at the staging post store too," said Abi, rummaging in her saddlebag.

"It's not more Tasty TNT, is it?" Josh asked.

Abi pulled out a bundle of paper and passed it over. "It's the *Daily Diplodocus*," she explained. "Got news about T-Bill."

Josh took the newspaper eagerly. Terrordactyl Bill was his all-time hero and the greatest dino wrangler the world had ever seen. His exploits were legendary, and Josh tried to model himself on T-Bill in every way, right down to his hat.

"T-Bill stopped a T. rex from trampling a town using just a tiny stick of dynamite!" he

read. "Says here the explosion discombobu-
lated the T. rex, which then ran away, leaving
the town completely safe. Wow!"

He was about to carry on when the paper was
snatched from his hands. Josh looked up into
the greasy, grinning face of his archenemy.

"Amos," he spat. "Give that back!"

Amos Wilks sneered as he weaved his club-
tailed ankylosaurus out of Josh's reach. "Says
here the explosion took out half of the town's
saloon," Amos read. "So much for leaving it safe!"

"Yeah," sniggered Amos's weasel-faced side-
kick, Arthur, who was scurrying along on his
own gallimimus. "So much for leaving it safe!"

"Shut up, Arthur," Amos snapped.

"Shutting up," said Arthur meekly.

"What do you know, Amos?" Josh asked, making another grab for the newspaper.

"I know plenty," Amos told him. "Fact is, I'm a better dino wrangler than T-Bill ever was. I could wrestle a T. rex to a standstill with my bare hands."

"With your bad breath, maybe," Abi muttered.

"I still don't get why you're here," Josh said. "You don't know anything about herding guanos."

"Maybe I just wanted to keep you company," said Amos. He tore the newspaper in half and let the wind carry it off. "And let you see what a *real* hero looks like."

"You?" Josh snorted. "You must be joking!"

"Guys?" said Sam.

12

"I'm stronger and braver than that stupid T-Bill any day!"

Josh growled. "You take that back."

"Guys, look!" Sam shouted. He pointed to where the guano herd had started to pull ahead. They were already at the narrow mountain pass—the only safe track leading through the Wandering Mountains. "We're falling behind."

"Last one there's a brontosaurus butt," Amos cried, kicking his ankylosaurus hard and sending it racing across the plain. Josh and the others hurried after him, and the booming of all five sets of dino feet shook the ground around them.

But that wasn't all that was shaking, Josh realized as they reached the edge of the mountain pass. Tiny pebbles were rolling and clattering down the hill beside him. A larger rock bounced off the ground with a *crack*.

Suddenly, there was a rumbling from up high—loud enough to be heard even over the footsteps and the low calls of the entire guano herd. Josh and the others rocked violently in their saddles as the ground beneath them shook.

Abi let out a sharp gasp, then pointed upward. A torrent of rocks and stones was tumbling and rolling down the mountainside toward them.

"Avalanche!" she cried.

"Well, technically, it's a landslide," Sam began.

But before Abi had a chance to call him a

smarty-pants, the rumbling continued, dust filled the air, and a whole slab of mountain came crashing toward them.

CHAPTER

2

J osh and the others leaned low in their saddles and powered along the narrow path, coughing and spluttering through the clouds of dust. A rock the size of Josh's head shattered on the ground right ahead. Charge dodged left to avoid it, and Josh yelped as he scraped against the rocky mountainside.

A hail of pebbles struck Abi on the back, stinging her through her rough shirt. Behind

her, Sam held on for dear life as his dinosaur leaped over a falling boulder, almost tossing him out of the saddle.

Somewhere through the dust cloud, Josh thought he could hear his dad shouting, but

the deafening roar of the landslide made it impossible to tell for sure. Josh waved his hand in front of his face, trying to make out what was up ahead, but the cloud was too thick to see more than a few meters.

From somewhere above, Josh heard a worrying *crack*, followed by the booming of something big and heavy tumbling down the mountainside toward him. He looked up and saw an enormous shadow plunging down through the dust. An enormous boulder was about to hit, and Charge was on a collision course!

Heaving back on the reins, Josh called out to his dino, "Stop!"

Charge planted his front feet and skidded

across the carpet of fallen pebbles. Josh grabbed onto the triceratops's armored fringe, his knuckles turning white as he clung on.

The triceratops slid to a stop, just as a rock the size of a baby bronto smashed down in front of him. The impact shook the hillsides, and Charge frantically backed away as first dozens then hundreds of smaller rocks came tumbling down behind it.

Sam, Abi, Amos, and Arthur arrived behind Josh just as the landslide stopped its sliding. When the dust settled, the path ahead was blocked by a towering wall of stone. With sheer mountain cliffs on both the left and the right, there was no way through.

"Oh, well, that's just great." Amos hissed.

"That's the only way through the Wandering Mountains."

"Yeah, nice one, Sanders," Arthur echoed.

Josh turned angrily in his saddle. "How is this my fault? If it wasn't for you two, we wouldn't have fallen behind."

"You nearly got us crushed," Abi told them. "We could have been pancaked."

"Not that it would have been much of a loss to the world," Amos barked back.

Josh was about to ready his lasso, but Sam jumped in.

"Perhaps we should save the arguing for later?" he suggested. "We need to figure out what to do."

"Josh?" A voice called out.

Dad's voice was faint and muffled, but Josh could just about hear it.

"We're OK, Dad!" Josh shouted back.

"Go home," his dad shouted. "I'll see you there in a couple of weeks."

Josh slumped in his saddle. "Aw, man," he groaned. "I wanted to go to Scaly Point."

Sam clambered off his dinosaur to inspect the scene. "There's no way we can get past this," he reported. "Looks like we have to turn back."

Josh shrugged. He'd been really looking forward to the trek. Now the five of them were on their own, and there was nothing they could do.

"I suppose," he began. "Unless anyone has a bright idea."

He looked around hopefully, but the others were silent. He yanked on Charge's reins to turn him around. Suddenly, Abi piped up.

"What if there's another way?" she said.

"There isn't," said Sam. "This is the only pass, unless we try to go over." He looked up at the snowcapped peaks towering above them and shivered. "And I don't want to go up there."

"Not up there," said Abi. All eyes turned to look at her as she pulled a crumpled map from her saddlebag and laid it across her dinosaur's back. She pointed to a patch of green beside two towering mountains. "Down. Through there."

Sam stood on his tiptoes to see the map, then let out a gasp. "You can't be serious?"

"It's that or go home," said Abi.

"Then I vote for going home," Sam blurted. "All in favor?"

He and Arthur both put their hands up at the same time. Amos let out a menacing growl, and Arthur quickly put his hand back down again.

Sam looked hopefully at the others, then lowered his own hand. "You do all understand what that place is, right? You do understand what we'd be getting into?"

Josh leaned over in Charge's saddle and nodded slowly as he studied the map. "Yup," he said in awe. "The Roaring Jaws Valley."

"Most dangerous place in the whole West, some say," Abi added.

"*Exactly!*" Sam yelled.

Amos sneered. "You scared?"

"Yes! Terrified!" said Sam. "We all should be. It's predator central. It's death city. It's where dino riders go to get eaten up and pooped out by giant toothy monsters!"

"But," Josh said, a smile creeping across his face, "we'd be able to get ahead of the others and meet them at the other end of the pass."

"Or we could be something's lunch," Sam pointed out.

"Come on, Sam," Josh said. "What would T-Bill do?"

Amos sneered and turned his ankylosaurus around. "Forget T-Bill. *I'm* a full-blown survival expert."

"You're a full-blown pain in the butt," Josh muttered.

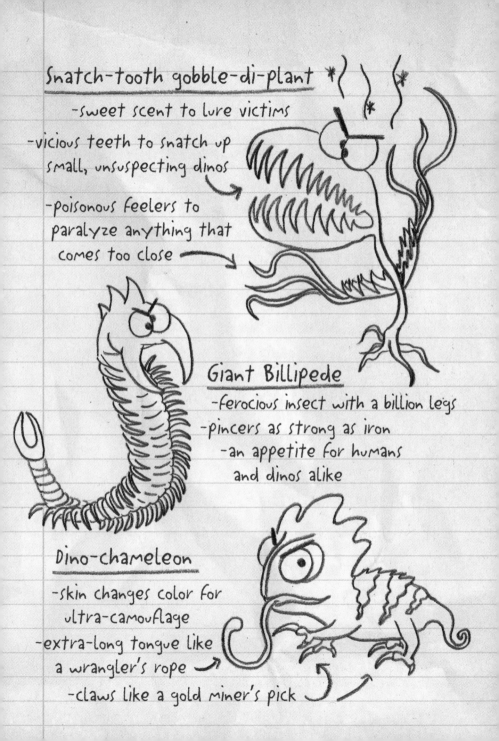

Snatch-tooth gobble-di-plant

   -sweet scent to lure victims

-vicious teeth to snatch up
small, unsuspecting dinos

   -poisonous feelers to
   paralyze anything that
   comes too close

Giant Billipede
   -ferocious insect with a billion legs
   -pincers as strong as iron
     -an appetite for humans
     and dinos alike

Dino-chameleon

-skin changes color for
   ultra-camouflage
-extra-long tongue like
   a wrangler's rope
   -claws like a gold miner's pick

Despite Sam's protests, the five of them eventually agreed to go through the Roaring Jaws Valley. They descended the winding, rock-strewn path they'd been on and made their way to a fork in the road. Hours of backtracking and a lot of twisting turns later, the dry, dusty valley was gone. In its place was a thick jungle of lush greenery, speckled with vibrant flowers of orange, purple, and every other color under the sun. Josh and the others sat bolt upright in their saddles in wonder.

Tangled vines trailed from towering treetops. Leaves almost as large as Arthur cast shadows on the knotted grass below. From deep within the jungle came the high-pitched chirping of bugs, birds, or both.

"It's incredible," Josh whispered as he led the others through a gap in the trees. They emerged into a narrow clearing and immediately felt like they were in a whole new world. The Roaring Jaws Valley was like a lost world.

"I've never seen anything like it," Abi said.

Even Sam seemed impressed, all fear of being gobbled up by a T. rex forgotten for the moment.

"It's not bad, I suppose," Amos begrudgingly admitted. "If you like that sort of thing."

"Sh!" Josh hissed.

Amos opened his mouth to spit out a reply, but then he heard it too. A rustling in the trees up ahead. Close—and getting closer.

"What is it?" Sam whispered as the rustling grew louder. "What's that noise?"

Josh peered into the dense foliage. "I don't know," he said. "But I think we're about to find out!"

CHAPTER 3

Josh reached for his lasso and held it loosely in his hands. He wanted to be ready. The rustling had become a crashing. Any second now, whatever was in there would explode into the clearing.

A shape shot out of the shadows. Amos let out a high-pitched squeal of terror, then frowned as Josh, Abi, and Sam burst out laughing.

"Dilongs!" Abi said, sliding down from her

saddle. Down on the ground, a dozen tiny dinos darted around on their spindly legs, chattering excitedly and fluttering their colorful feathers. They looked almost exactly like T. rexes, but since they were only two feet tall, they were nowhere near as scary. Abi bent down to pat one on its soft, downy head.

"Aw, look at the little fella," she said.

"Stay back, Amos," Sam said, grinning. "We wouldn't want you getting scared."

"Shut it, dweeb." Amos scowled. "I wasn't scared."

"Yeah, right. You just screamed like that for fun," Abi said, tickling one of the little dinosaurs under its feathery chin. It made a happy purring sound.

"Maybe the Roaring Jaws Valley isn't so bad after all," said Sam.

Josh nodded but peered into the shadowy jungle again. Those dilongs sure had been in a hurry. Almost like they'd been running away from something...

"Yeah," he said. "Maybe not."

"I wonder if they'd like this," said Sam, tipping some Tasty TNT into his palm. He held it out to one of the dilongs. It gave the candy an experimental sniff and then lapped up the powder with its pointed tongue.

For a moment, nothing happened. The dilong just stood there, tongue flicking inside its mouth. But then...

Whoosh! The dilong leaped straight up into

the air, flipped over once, and landed on its face. It jumped up again, screeching and squawking as it ran in circles, its tongue flailing wildly around outside its mouth.

It made a dash for the trees again, thumped straight into one, then finally vanished into the undergrowth.

Sam glanced at Josh and the others. "Don't think he was a fan," he said sheepishly.

The other dilongs eyed Sam warily, then set off after their friend. The children all mounted up and continued on through the dense jungle. Josh led the way on his triceratops, using Charge's horns and armored head to clear a path.

"Looking at the map, we should make it

through to the other side by tomorrow night," Abi said.

"Tomorrow night?" repeated Sam. "But that's a whole day away!"

"Whoa, check out the big brain on you," said Amos from near the back of the line. "How *did* you figure that out all by yourself?"

"It's OK, Sam," said Josh. "We'll ride for a couple more hours, then find somewhere to rest."

"Outside?" Sam asked anxiously. "Dilongs are one thing, but there are supposed to be T. rexes and all sorts in here."

"Yeah, hungry ones," said Amos, sniggering.

"Just rumors," Abi assured him. "The last actual sighting was years ago."

"That's because no one since then has

survived to tell the tale," Amos said. He laughed as he heard Sam gulp nervously.

"Don't listen to him, Sam," Abi said and sighed. "Look, there's a clearing a couple of hours from here. We'll just..." She stopped. "Hey, wait," she said.

Josh glanced back over his shoulder. "What is it?"

"There's a settlement," Abi said. She brought the map closer to her face and squinted. "Real small, but it's definitely a settlement. A little town or a few ranches maybe. I can't tell for sure."

Sam's eyes widened. "A settlement? That means beds! And walls! And not having to sleep outside! Let's go there."

"Fine by me," said Josh.

"It'll be safer with more folks around," Abi agreed.

Amos puffed out his chest. "Well, if you babies are too scared to camp out under the stars, then I guess I'll have to come too. Don't want you getting lost."

"Yeah," agreed Arthur, who was trotting along at the very back of the line. "What he said."

"Then it's settled," said Josh. "Mystery settle-ment, here we come."

As they trekked on through the jungle, Josh marveled at the sights, smells, and sounds around them. Strangely shaped fruit hung from high branches. Odd little insects wriggled on tree stumps or fluttered around their faces.

Every few miles, they'd come across another pack of dilongs or other small dinosaurs, which quickly scattered when Charge's head pushed through the trees beside them.

As well, the air in the valley felt different. Back home, it was dry as a bone, but here, it was hot and heavy with moisture. Their drinking water was long gone, and the pressing heat was making them sweat and pant.

"I think we're close to the stream," Abi called, looking at her map.

Sure enough, just a few paces farther on, the trees thinned out a little. There, cutting a trench through the undergrowth, was a stream of sparkling blue water.

They didn't even stop to dismount. Instead,

they hurried into the stream on their dinos, laughing as the great beasts' feet kicked up a cool spray of water. They scooped up handfuls of water and drank. The icy-cool liquid felt like a taste explosion in Josh's mouth. Not a horribly sour taste explosion like Sam's Tasty TNT, thankfully. The water was one of the most delicious things he'd ever tasted, second only to his mom's famous pterodactyl-egg pie.

Once they'd all drunk their fill, they dipped their water bottles into the stream and filled those too. "Settlement's just ahead," Abi said.

"Then what are we waiting for?" cried Sam, thoughts of a comfortable bed and a safe place to sleep filling his head. "Let's go!"

The dinos scrambled up the side of the muddy

bank, and the children followed the curve of the stream. As the trees cleared, they saw a wooden signpost creaking in the breeze.

A Warm Welcome to Toothy Gulch.

They hurried past the sign, and the trees opened onto a wide clearing. There, standing ahead of them, was a small town made up of houses, stores, a saloon, and even a bank. It was almost as big as Trihorn settle-ment back home.

Together, all five children rode their dinos onto the main street. It was neatly kept, the long grass of the jungle covered over by carefully constructed flagstone roads and paths. It looked like a real nice place to live. There was just one problem.

"Where is everyone?" Josh asked, looking around. There were no dinos tethered outside the saloon. No people going about their day. Nothing.

"Hello?" Abi called, but the only reply was the echo of her voice bouncing back at her from the nearby mountainside.

Hopping down from Charge's back, Josh tied the dino to a tethering post, then headed for the saloon. The swinging doors creaked as he pushed them open and stepped inside.

The saloon was empty, but by the looks of

it, it hadn't been empty for long. Half-finished drinks sat on the tables. Poker chips were piled up alongside a few hands of cards that had been abandoned midgame.

Over on the bar, a curl of smoke rose lazily from the burned-down stub of a cigar.

"So much for the warm welcome," Josh whispered. "Toothy Gulch is a ghost town!"

CHAPTER 4

The next morning, Josh opened his eyes and gazed up at the cobwebs in the corner of the room. He was on the hard, wooden floor of the saloon's bedroom. Amos and Arthur had gone off to find their own rooms, even though he'd suggested sticking together for safety.

"Anyone awake?" Josh whispered.

Abi turned over in her sleeping bag. "Yeah."

From up on the bed came the sound of Sam snoring. Abi and Josh had agreed to let him have the comfiest spot, if only so they didn't have to listen to him complaining all the next day.

"Sam!" Abi said with a hiss.

Sam sat bolt upright. "Wha—? What's wrong?"

"Are you awake?" Abi asked.

Sam yawned. "Well, I am now!"

Wriggling out of his sleeping bag, Josh stretched, then crossed to the window. The main street of Toothy Gulch was just as deserted as it had been yesterday. Charge was tied up at a tethering post right outside the saloon, alongside Sam, Abi, and Arthur's gallimimuses. Amos's ankylosaurus, Clubber, was tethered by himself down the street, so he couldn't pick a fight with the others.

"Come on, let's go get Amos and Arthur," Josh said, turning from the window.

"So we can get out of here?" asked Sam hopefully.

"So we can figure out what's going on!" said Josh.

Sam groaned. "I thought you might say that."

Twenty minutes later, the children all sat around a table, sipping sarsaparilla from the saloon's cracked glasses. Amos was fiddling with some poker chips, passing them noisily from hand to hand as Josh talked.

"The way I see it, we have two choices," Josh said, trying to ignore the clicking of the chips.

"We can look around and try to figure out what's going on, or we can keep going, get out of the valley, then meet up with the herd."

"I vote we look around," said Amos.

"So you can see if there's anything worth stealing?" asked Josh. "If we do look around, we'll be keeping a close eye on you, Amos."

Amos snarled but didn't say any more. Arthur tried to snarl too, but instead of being threatening, it just looked like he was holding back a sneeze.

"What happened to everyone?" Abi asked. "People don't just up and disappear."

"It's a mining town," said Sam. "Perhaps all the gold ran out."

"So what, they just got up and left mid-drink?"

asked Josh, pointing at the abandoned glasses on the tables around them.

"Maybe they got lost," Arthur volunteered. All eyes turned to look at him, and he blushed slightly. "I do that sometimes—go out, then forget where I live."

There was a moment of silence. Everyone blinked at the same time.

"Shut up, Arthur," Amos said and scowled.

"Maybe they breached a pocket of gas while mining," said Sam, suddenly looking worried. "What if there's a toxic gas leak, and everyone had to flee? What if we're breathing it in right now?"

He held his breath until his face turned bright purple and swelled up like a balloon.

Abi poked his cheek, forcing him to breathe out again.

"We've been here for hours," she pointed out. "We'd have noticed if we were breathing poisonous gas."

Amos laughed and slapped the table so hard, he made everyone jump in fright.

"What's so funny?" Josh asked.

"The answer is right in front of you," he said. "You do know they're called *ghost towns* for a reason." He leaned forward in his chair, like he was about to reveal a big secret. "You ever hear the story of Sheriff Shackles?" he asked. "He was the lawman around these parts. A crooked one, always helping himself to what other folks had."

Gold Creek

Famous gold mining town that grew wealthy in the Lost Plains gold rush. Abandoned when miners discovered underground dinosaurs that feasted on humans like bedtime snacks. The ghosts of the miners still haunt the caves now...

Lynchfield Brooks

A town that was overrun by escaped convicts, which became cut off from the Lost Plains by an icy winter. The ghosts of the criminals still wander through the icy valley, robbing folk who stray too near.

"A hero of yours, was he?" Josh asked.

Amos just ignored him. "Slim Jim Shackleton they called him, on account of him being a skinny fella. Named Jim. Course, that was before he died in a shoot-out."

A hush fell across the table. "He died?" Arthur asked.

"Yup," said Amos, nodding slowly. "But he didn't stay dead for long. Not all the way dead, at least. He came back, all pale and dusty-like. They say his ghost roams Roaring Jaws Valley, riding around on the back of his ghostly T. rex, Spook, imprisoning anyone he meets right here in the town jail."

"You made all that up," said Josh.

"Nope, it's all true. Every word," Amos insisted. "Sheriff Shackles locks folks up in his cells, then leaves them there until they're nothing but ghosts themselves."

Sam swallowed nervously, and Abi loosened her collar. Silence descended on the room.

"Perhaps we should press on to meet the herd," Sam suggested.

"Don't listen to him, Sam," Josh said. "He's just trying to scare us."

"Oh really?" said Amos. "Well, if you're so sure I'm lying, why don't we go check out the jail and see who's right?"

"Fine!" said Josh, standing up. "I'll prove there's nothing there, then we can be on our way."

"Maybe," said Amos, grinning. "Unless Sheriff Shackles catches you…"

The jailhouse door creaked as it swung inward into the dark, dusty room beyond. Josh hesitated outside it, peering into the gloom. He thought he didn't believe Amos's story, but the way his heart had started racing told him that maybe, deep down, he did. Sam and Abi were bunched up close behind him. Sam looked terrified, and even Abi wasn't her usual confident self.

"What's the matter? Too scared to go inside?" Amos asked with a snort from behind them.

Josh shot a glare back over his shoulder, took a steadying breath, then stepped through into the jailhouse.

The jail was just as empty as everywhere else in town. There was no sheriff—ghostly or otherwise—and no spooks or spirits floating around in any of the four cells. The doors to the cells stood open, suggesting either they hadn't been used in a while or the prisoners had all been set free in a hurry.

"Nothing here," said Josh. "Told you."

"Not these cells," Amos whispered. He pointed to a set of narrow steps at the far end of the room. "The cells in the basement."

"Oh good," Sam croaked. "Checking for ghosts in a creepy basement. What could go wrong?"

They crept down the wooden staircase in a chorus of creaks and groans. It was much darker now, with only the light from a tiny, narrow window to push away the shadows. They could just make out three more cells in the gloom. To Sam's relief, they were all empty too.

"See? Completely ghost

free," said Josh, but he couldn't hide the shake in his voice. He frowned as he spotted something on the wall at the back of one of the cells. "Wait, what's this?"

The friends kept close together as they crept into the cell and studied the wall. Scratchy letters had been carved into the bricks. The darkness made it difficult to work out what it said, but after studying it for a while, Josh was able to figure it out.

"Slim Jim Shackleton was here," he read.

Then, reading further down, "Look behind you."

The three friends exchanged a nervous glance, but before they could turn, there was a deafening *clang* as the door to the cell slammed shut!

Josh, Sam, and Abi spun around, expecting to see a spooky sheriff floating in the air above the scuffed wooden floor. Instead, they saw something worse: Amos's grinning face.

"Oh man, I can't believe you fell for that!" Amos laughed. "You should see your faces!"

Josh grabbed the bars of the cells and rattled them. The door didn't budge. "Let us out, Amos," he demanded. "Joke's over!"

Amos shook his head. "Joke's over when I say it's over, runt," he spat. "Reckon we'll leave you in there for a few hours. Arthur and I will go and cook us up some breakfast, then have a good nose around without anyone's prying eyes keeping watch over us. Maybe then we'll come back and let you out. Maybe."

Abi thrust an arm through the bars, grabbing for Amos, but he skipped back and laughed again. "Nice try! Oh, and I hope you all went to the bathroom this morning," he said, pointing to a rusted bucket in the corner of the cell. "The facilities in here are kinda basic."

The three friends all hollered after Amos and Arthur as they turned and ran up the stairs. They stopped shouting when they heard the front door slam and the scuffing of the bullies' feet on the stone path outside.

"He's locked us in!" said Sam as if only just realizing this.

"Yeah, we noticed," said Abi. "Now what do we do?"

Josh sighed. "I guess there's not much we can do but wait. Starting to wish we'd eaten breakfast before we came out."

"Oh, wait! I can help with that," said Sam. "I've got food!"

"Awesome!" Josh cheered. His and Abi's bellies rumbled hungrily as Sam fished in his bulging pockets. A moment later, Sam pulled out several paper bags in each hand.

"I've got enough Tasty TNT to last us all day!" he announced.

Josh groaned. "That stuff? I think I'd rather go hungry!"

"Yeah," agreed Abi. "Me too. It nearly dissolved my teeth."

Sam shrugged and stuffed the bags back in his

pockets. Josh tried rattling the bars of the cell again, in case they magically opened this time. They didn't. He tried to think about what T-Bill would do in this situation. He quickly came to the conclusion that T-Bill wouldn't have fallen for the trick in the first place.

"What was that?" Sam whispered.

Josh turned away from the door. "What was what?"

"It got very cold in here, just for a moment," Sam said. He glanced nervously around the darkened basement. He'd read enough books to know what a sudden chill could mean. "Maybe Amos wasn't kidding about the ghost!" he whimpered. "Maybe it's in here with us *right n-now*."

"Of course he was kidding. You probably just imagined it," said Abi, then she froze as a wave of cold air washed over her too. "No, wait. I felt it."

"See!" Sam squeaked. "We're doomed."

Josh frowned. He'd felt the cold air too, but he didn't think there was anything supernatural about it. Dropping to his knees, he held his hands above a gap between two of the floor's wooden planks. Sure enough, a breeze was blowing through it.

"Guys, help me lift this up," he said, squeezing his fingers into the gap and pulling on the plank. With Sam and Abi's help, he lifted the plank free, revealing a tunnel underneath!

"So much for justice in Toothy Gulch," he

said. "The jail comes with its very own escape tunnel!"

Josh led the way, squeezing through the hole and dropping down into the narrow space. The tunnel wasn't very deep, so he had to crawl along on all fours, but a light at the far end meant they could at least see where they were going.

The ground was made of packed soil, with the odd tree root weaving through it. It hurt Josh's knees, but after less than a minute of crawling up the steep slope, he emerged into the fresh air in the middle of a clump of prickly bushes.

"Ooh, ow, ouch," he muttered, fighting his way out of the scrub. He held the thorny branches aside as best he could while Sam and Abi clambered free.

Once they were all back aboveground, they spent a few minutes picking the barbed thorns out of their skin. "Let's go find Amos and Arthur," Josh said, tearing the final prickle free. "Those two won't know what hit them."

"Yes, they will," said Abi, gritting her teeth and clenching her fists. "Me!"

CHAPTER 6

Running out from behind the jailhouse, Josh and the others immediately spotted smoke curling up from the chimney of the saloon. Josh could smell the unmistakable aroma of sizzling guano sausages and knew that Amos and Arthur must be cooking breakfast.

"They're in here," Josh said, marching along Main Street and throwing open the saloon's swinging doors.

Sure enough, they followed the smell and found Amos and Arthur in the smoke-filled kitchen, coughing and spluttering as their breakfast burned and turned black in a pan on the stove.

Arthur made a grab for the pan's metal handle. There was a loud *hiss* from his hand, and he leaped away, squealing as he hopped from foot to foot. "Ooh, hot, hot!" he yelped.

"Don't be such a baby," Amos said. He grabbed the handle and lifted the pan, then squealed as it burned his hand. He let the pan drop to the floor, and a burst of flame flowered up from the wooden floorboards.

Amos and Arthur ran from the fire, which had already started to creep across the floor. Thinking fast, Josh snatched a towel from a rail, plunged it into the half-full washbasin, and used it to whip and beat back the blaze. He stamped out the last few flames, then dropped the damp towel over the sizzling pan.

"Oh, well done, Sanders," Amos said with a scowl, pressing his sore hand under his arm. "You ruined breakfast."

"It was pretty ruined before Josh got anywhere near it," said Abi.

"Yeah, you could've burned the place to the ground!" Josh said.

"We had it under control," Amos said. Behind him, Arthur continued to whimper and hop from foot to foot. "Mostly." He looked Josh up and down. "How come you're here, anyway? You should still be locked up."

"We got out," said Abi.

"We escaped from an underground prison cell. You two can't even make breakfast," Josh said. "So much for being a survival expert."

"You wouldn't stand a chance out there without us," crowed Amos. He stepped in close to Josh, using his hulking size to try to intimidate him.

"Well, we'll find out," Josh said. He stretched as tall as he could, but the top of his head still barely came up to Amos's chin.

"We're going to head off to meet the herd. You two can fend for yourselves. Let's see how you cope without *us*."

"Ha! You won't last five minutes," said Amos.

"You mean you won't," said Josh.

"No, I mean *you*." Amos growled, bending so he and Josh were almost nose to nose.

"Yeah, but really you mean *you*," Josh snarled.

"You!"

"You!"

"This is getting us nowhere!" Abi snapped, getting between them. "Amos, you're lucky I don't knock your head off for chucking us in that jail cell. Josh is right. You two are on your own. We don't need you."

"Yes, you do," Amos said.

"Do not!" insisted Josh.

"Do too!"

"Cut it out!" said Abi, raising her voice to be heard over the sound of their bickering. "Come on, guys, we're leaving," she said, turning toward the door. As she did, she caught a glimpse of something moving outside the window. A shadow flitted across the glass.

"What was that?" whispered Sam, who had spotted the shadow too.

"There's someone out there," Abi said, her voice now low and quiet.

"Or something," Sam added.

Abi tiptoed to the kitchen door and peeked out. The saloon's bar area was still exactly as empty as before. She, Sam, and Josh snuck out of the kitchen. Even Amos and Arthur tried to keep as quiet as possible as they followed behind.

"Is this a joke?" Amos demanded. "If you're going to try to get us back for the jail cell, then it's not going to work. We're way smarter than you."

"I've met brontosaurus eggs smarter than you are, Amos," Abi whispered. "But it's not a trick. There was definitely something moving out there, and I don't think it was a pack of dilongs."

"Listen!" said Josh. From outside, there came the steady *clomp-clomp-clomp* of feet on the wooden walkway right outside the saloon. Someone was approaching slowly, getting closer and closer with each thudding step.

"Who is it?" asked Sam. "Who's out there?"

They didn't have to wait long to find out. The saloon door swung inward on its creaky hinges, and there, framed in the doorway, was a pale and dusty figure with a hat pulled down low on his head. There was a star-shaped badge pinned to his coat. Across it was written just a single word.

Sheriff.

Josh's jaw dropped, and his eyes went wide. He was real. The ghost of Sheriff Shackles was real.

And he'd found them!

CHAPTER 7

The frightening figure took a pace inside the room, letting the doors swing closed behind him. Josh and the others backed away, eyes widening.

"Well now," said the sheriff in a voice as dry and withered as dead leaves. "What have we here?"

He took another pace forward,

his wrinkled hands reaching out for them. Josh and the others spun on the spot and made a frantic scramble for the stairs leading up to the bedrooms.

"Get out of my way!" Amos squealed, elbowing the others aside. "D-don't let the ghost get me!"

They clambered up the steps, hurled themselves into the closest bedroom, and slammed the door. There was a rusted slide-bolt screwed into the wood. Josh's hands shook as he fumbled with it and finally slid it closed.

A moment later, there was a knocking on the door. Josh reached for his lasso, holding it ready at his side. Abi stood next to him, with Sam partly tucked in behind her. Amos and

Arthur, meanwhile, dropped to the floor and climbed under the bed.

Knock. Knock. Knock.

"I know you're in there," called the voice from outside. "Open up."

Knock. Knock. Knock.

"What do we do?" whispered Abi.

"I could try to lasso him," Josh said.

"Lasso a ghost?" scoffed Sam. "The rope will pass right through!"

Josh glanced down at the coiled lasso, then up at the door. "Hey, that's a good point. Why isn't he floating through the door?"

"Sh! Keep your voice down," Sam urged. "You don't want to give him ideas."

The door handle rattled, making them all

jump. There was a loud *thud* as the sheriff hurled himself against the wood on the other side. "Open up, or I'm coming in anyway!" he called.

Josh hooked his rope back onto his belt. "I think we should let him in," he said.

"Are you crazy?" yelped Amos from under the bed. "It's Sheriff Shackles! He'll lock us all up."

"OK, firstly, I'm not so sure it is Sheriff Shackles," said Josh. "And secondly, Amos, tough guys aren't supposed to hide under the bed."

"I ain't hiding," said Amos. "I'm...taking cover. There's a big difference!"

With a crack, the door exploded inward, and the sheriff came stumbling into the room, shoulder first.

"Wah!" he yelled, off-balance. He fell to the

floor, rolled forward, and then sprang back to his feet, all without losing his hat. "Phew. That was close," the sheriff said. He dusted himself off, then looked at Josh and the others. "Who are you?" he demanded.

"W-who are you?" asked Sam. "Are you a g-ghost?"

The sheriff gave a confused smile, then looked Sam up and down. "Uh, not that I know of," he said. He pushed his hat back, revealing a weather-beaten face with a drooping white moustache and eyes that seemed to twinkle.

"You're not Sheriff Shackles?" asked Abi.

"Never heard of him. Sheriff Withers is the name. I'm the lawman for Toothy Gulch." He tapped the shiny star on his chest as Amos and

Arthur began to wriggle out from under the bed. "You kids shouldn't be here. It's dangerous," the sheriff said.

"Where is everyone?" asked Josh.

"Up in the mountains, not far from here," said Sheriff Withers. "I was on my way back for supplies when I saw the smoke from the chimney. Reckoned I'd best come take a look and see who was in here. Mighty glad that I did."

"I still don't understand," said Josh. "Why did everyone leave? What are they doing up in the mountains."

"Hiding," said the sheriff.

"Hiding?" asked Josh. "Hiding from what?"

Boom!

The saloon shook. From outside, Josh heard

Charge and the other dinosaurs whinny and bray anxiously.

Boom!

A framed painting of a brontosaurus-filled landscape trembled, then fell off the wall. Amos and Arthur both glanced at the bed again, like they were considering jumping under there.

Abi raised a shaking finger and pointed it toward the window. "I'm guessing they're hiding from th-that!" she said.

Josh and the others turned to the window. There, glaring in at them through the glass, was an enormous bloodshot yellow eye. It swiveled as it scanned the room, its dark pupil narrowing. Josh had never seen one this close before—he doubted anyone had and lived to

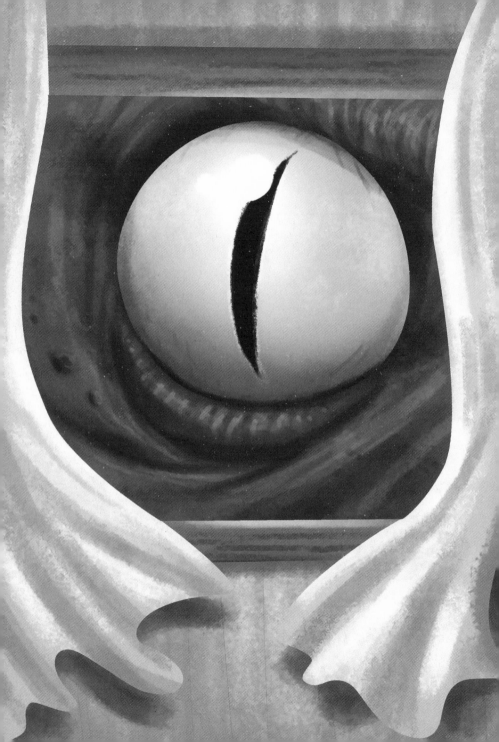

talk about it—but he recognized that eyeball. It was the eyeball of a tyrannosaurus rex!

"Yup," whispered Sheriff Withers. "That's what we been hiding from, all right."

"Nobody move," Amos squeaked. "T. rexes can only see stuff that's moving."

Josh slowly shook his head. He'd spent his whole life gathering facts about dinosaurs and writing them down in his journal. Fact was, he knew pretty much everything there was to know about any dinosaur out there, the T. rex included.

He knew what they liked to eat.

He knew how fast they could move.

He knew that the enormous flesh eater on the other side of the glass could see them just fine.

And he knew that there was only one thing they could do.

"Run!"

CHAPTER 8

The T. rex lunged forward. Its head smashed through the wooden wall, razor-sharp teeth snapping hungrily through the air. Suddenly, Josh and the others were surrounded by the warm, choking stench of the dinosaur's breath as they stumbled across the hallway, tumbled down the steps, then landed in a heap at the bottom.

"Move!" barked the sheriff, struggling to his

feet and running for the saloon's front door. The others scrambled after him, just as the T. rex's tail erupted through the staircase, turning it to splinters.

"Follow me to the bank!" Sheriff Withers said. "We'll get inside the vault. It's the safest place in town."

"You all go. I've got to untie the dinos first!" Josh cried, racing over to where Charge and the others were tethered. The gallimimuses were bucking and braying with fear, but Charge was standing glaring at the T. rex, his head lowered and ready to fight.

"Don't even think about it, buddy," Josh told him, frantically untying the knots holding the dinosaurs in place and gathering up the rope. The other dinos fled at once, but Charge stood his ground, breath snorting from his nostrils.

Charge looked up at the T. rex just as it whipped its tail around, smashing it through the side of the saloon. Splinters of wood and rusted nails rained down around Josh and his

dinosaur. Charge lowered his head and tensed his shoulders.

"Charge, don't!" Josh cried, but it was too late. The brave triceratops broke into a run, aiming for one of the tyrannosaurus's legs with his horns. The T. rex's tail whipped again. Josh could only watch as the rest of the saloon came crashing down on top of his dino.

"No!" Josh howled. Charge was nowhere to be seen.

He took a few steps toward the fallen building, but the ground shook, and a furious roar rolled all the way along the street as the T. rex rounded on him.

"Josh, hurry!" Abi hollered as she and Sam untied the rope tethering Amos's dinosaur.

Sheriff Withers was already in the doorway of the bank, calling for Josh to follow.

Another thunderous footstep made the whole town shudder. Abi grabbed Josh's arm and yanked him away from the wreckage.

"No, wait!" he cried.

But it was too late. The T. rex was on him. The giant beast opened its giant jaws and roared, its gross dino saliva drenching him and Abi. There was no choice. He had to leave Charge and hope the triceratops was OK.

Lowering his head, Josh powered on alongside Abi. The bank was only twenty meters ahead now, but the thudding of the T. rex's feet was coming faster.

"Get inside!" Josh wheezed. "Go!"

Abi bolted ahead and joined the others.

Josh glanced behind him as the T. rex's jaws gnashed and bit. He hurtled toward the bank, then launched himself inside.

"In here!" Sheriff Withers cried, and they all linked hands as he pulled them into the bank's enormous vault.

The T. rex's head tore through the front of the building like a giant battering ram, turning the wall and part of the roof into little more than matchsticks. It made a lunge for Josh and the others, its jaw wide enough that they could see right down into its cavernous throat. Each tooth was bigger than Josh's whole body, and chunks of rotten meat were wedged in tight between them. A choking stench of things long dead rolled out of its mouth as it made a lunging snap right for them.

Clang!

The dinosaur's snout struck the vault. The vault shook just enough to make Amos and Arthur both scream in terror, but the metal held securely. Josh and the rest of the group moved right to the back of the vault as the T. rex tried again and again to force its head through the narrow doorway.

"Reckon we're safe here," said Sheriff Withers. "For the time being."

Josh nodded. "Hey, Amos," he began. "Now might be a good time to show off them T. rex wrangling skills of yours."

Everyone turned to look at Amos, who chose that moment to burst into floods of tears.

"Yeah," said Josh. "Thought not."

The T. rex drew back. They heard the ground shake under its feet again. "It's leaving." Sam whispered.

Josh shook his head. "Don't think so. It's sizing the place up. Looking for a weakness."

"And w-will it find one?" stammered Arthur, using his sleeve to wipe the nose of the sniveling Amos.

"Don't need to," said the sheriff. "Knows we'll have to come out of here sooner or later."

Josh began to pace up and down the vault. He needed a plan. What would T-Bill do? He'd have a handy stick of dynamite he could blow the T. rex up with! All Josh had available in the vault was some rope, a few stacks of money, and five or six bars of gold. He wondered briefly if the T. rex would accept a bribe.

He had his lasso, of course, but roping a beast that size was impossible. There had to be some way to stop it.

"Think, Josh," he muttered. "Think."

His eyes fell on Sam's bulging pockets. He stopped pacing. A smile slowly began to spread across his face. "Sam, empty your pockets," he said. "I need your candy!"

"Now's not the time for a snack!" Sam protested.

"Just do it!" Josh urged.

Sam did as he was told, and soon, seventeen

paper bags were spread out on the floor in front of Josh. He kept aside the bags of Tasty TNT popping sherbet and tipped the other candy onto the floor. They were mostly all hard, oblong-shaped, and very sticky. Lots of them had stuck together in the bag, and Josh set to work squashing all the others together too.

"What are you doing?" Abi asked.

"I'm doing what T-Bill would do," Josh explained. "I'm making an explosive that's gonna knock this dinosaur's butt into next week!"

Once he had stuck all the hard candies together, Josh was left with a sticky ball of sweets bigger than his head. Tearing open the bags of Tasty TNT, he poured the stuff all over the candy ball's sticky surface.

"What in tarnation do you plan on doing with that?" asked the sheriff, pushing back his hat and scratching his head.

"Watch," said Josh. He yanked open the door of the vault before anyone could stop him and raced out into the remains of the street.

"Hey, down here!" he hollered.

"He's lost his mind!" Sam whimpered.

"We need to get him back in here," Abi said.

Before she could move though, the T. rex's head lowered until it was hovering right above Josh.

Josh swallowed nervously as he watched the dinosaur's nostrils flare in and out. A rumbling growl rolled out of its throat. "C'mon," Josh whispered, holding the candy ball ready. "Open up."

But the T. rex kept its mouth firmly shut. It lowered its head until Josh was breathing in its hot, stinking breath. He thought maybe this wasn't such a great plan after all.

Suddenly, something slammed into the T. rex's leg, and Josh caught a glimpse of three sharp horns.

"Charge! You're OK!"

The tyrannosaurus drew back and let out a roar of pain. Josh saw his chance. Taking aim, he tossed the ball of candy into the dino's gaping jaws. Instinctively, it snapped its mouth shut, and the candy crunched between its deadly teeth.

For a moment, nothing happened. But then, the T. rex's bloodshot eyes went wide and bulged outward in their sockets. A volcano of yellow foam erupted from its mouth and dribbled between its teeth. Steam oozed out of its nostrils like clouds of fizzing snot. The T. rex tried to roar, but all that came out was a frightened whimper instead.

The popping and fizzing of the candy in the T. rex's mouth was so loud, they could hear it in the vault. The big beast lumbered in a circle, frantically trying to paw at its head with its tiny arms.

Josh seized his chance. He bundled up the rope from the vault and tied it around the T. rex's ankle. Then he hauled the rope around the dinosaur's other leg and pulled as hard as he could.

With a mighty crash, the T. rex fell onto its side, a trail of foamy yellow fizz coating the ground beside it.

"Well, I'll be a raptor's uncle," said Sheriff Withers. "You've only gone and hog-tied that rex! How in Roaring Jaws Valley did you do that?"

"Easy," Josh said and grinned. "Tasty TNT. You should try it sometime."

"It really is good!" Sam added, giving Josh a hearty slap on the back.

"And I couldn't have done it without Charge's help," he added as his dino pal trotted over to join them.

"Well, way I see it, you're both heroes," said the sheriff. "Toothy Gulch is saved, thanks to your quick thinking. And we got ourselves a tourist attraction. This big boy is gonna put Toothy Gulch on the map—make no mistake."

The foaming-mouthed T. rex rolled an eye in the sheriff's direction.

"Fact is, I'd go as far as to say that Terrordactyl Bill couldn't have done it better himself," the sheriff continued.

Josh smiled at the mention of T-Bill but suddenly realized the time.

"Guys," he began. "We were supposed to be on the other side of this valley by now. We gotta get going!"

The children corralled their dinos, calmed the still sobbing Amos down a little, said their good-byes to Sheriff Withers, and trotted out of the valley. They stepped onto the path just in time to meet the herd, where Josh's dad gaped at them all in amazement.

"What…?" he spluttered. "I mean… How?"

"We took a shortcut," Josh said, giving his dad a hug. "Through Roaring Jaws Valley."

Mr. Sanders gasped. "Roaring Jaws? But that place is dangerous!"

Josh shot his friends a smile. "Is it?" he asked. "Can't say we noticed."

Then he fell into step beside his dad and continued on their way to Scaly Point.

At the front this time.

Don't miss Josh's next adventure in
How to Catch a Dino Thief

CHAPTER 1

Josh crouched left in the saddle, steering his triceratops, Charge, around a jagged rocky outcrop. Charge's enormous feet thundered across the dusty ground as he hurtled through the twists and turns of the Roaring Jaws Valley.

"Yah!" Josh shouted over the booming of Charge's footsteps and the roaring of the T. rexes on either side. "Go, Charge, go!"

Josh spun in the saddle and looked back. Right behind him, his all-time hero, Terrordactyl Bill, raced along on his own fully grown triceratops. T-Bill gave Josh an encouraging nod, then flicked the reins of his dinosaur. He and Josh dodged and weaved side by side through the maze of rocks and boulders as the snapping jaws of the T. rex army drew closer!

"Giddyap!" Josh snapped his lasso at the closest tyrannosaurus, and the brute jumped back in fright.

"Good idea, partner!" cheered T-Bill, unhooking his own rope from his belt and cracking the air in front of another of the beasts. The tyrannosaur turned, spinning its long tail around like a whip.

Josh looked up ahead to where the landscape widened out into an open plain. They were nearly through the dangerous valley, but something was blocking the way. The whole end of the valley was lost in a cloud of…

Uh-oh.

As the wind whistled around him, Josh realized what he and T-Bill were running straight into. "Tornado!" he yelled, but it was too late! A swirling cloud of sand was lifted up into the air, choking him, blinding him, and scratching at his skin.

Josh turned, holding up his arms to protect himself. "T-Bill?" he cried, but his voice was swallowed by the storm. "Where are you?"

The whistling sound rose to a scream. Josh

peered up through the sand cloud and could just make out a tall tower spinning toward him. The wind hit Josh with the force of a charging triceratops. It wrenched him from the saddle and…

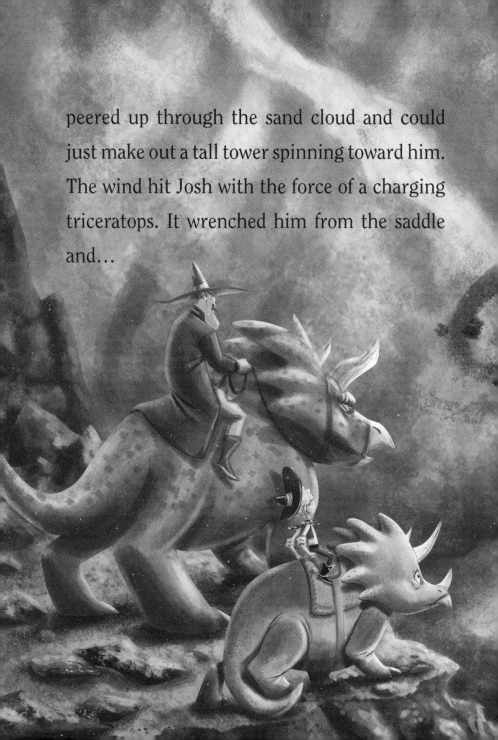

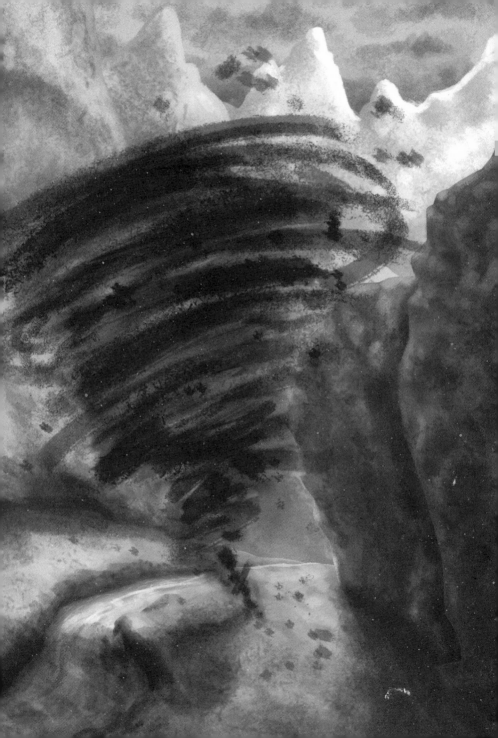

ABOUT THE AUTHOR

Ever since he was a little boy, Will Dare has been mad about T. rexes and velociraptors. He always wondered what it would be like to live in a world where they were still alive. Now, grown up, he has put pen to paper and imagined just that world. Will lives in rural America with his wife and his best pal, Charge (a dog, not a triceratops).